WALT DISNEY'S Bambi

Based on the original story
by Felix Salten

A GOLDEN BOOK • NEW YORK

Western Publishing Company, Inc., Racine, Wisconsin

One spring morning, in a little hidden forest glade, a fawn was born. All the birds and animals came to see him, for he was a very special fawn.

"What will you name the young Prince?" asked Thumper the rabbit.

"I will call him Bambi," the mother answered.

The forest was filled with friends. The opossums and
squirrels and robins and wrens all said, "Hello, young Prince!"
when Bambi walked down the leafy paths with his mother.
And Thumper and Flower the skunk came out to play with
Bambi nearly every day.

One morning Bambi's mother took him down a path where he had never been. At the end of the path was a wide green meadow.

What a wonderful place the meadow was! There was so much room to run and jump. Bambi leaped into the air three, four, five times.

When he stopped to catch his breath, another fawn came up to him. "Hello," she said softly.

Bambi tried to hide behind his mother.

"Don't be afraid, Bambi," she said. "This is Faline. Her mother is your Aunt Ena."

Soon Bambi and Faline were racing around the meadow together.

Suddenly they heard hoofbeats. A herd of stags came galloping across the meadow, led by the great Prince of the Forest.

The great Prince was older and bigger and stronger than the other stags, and he was very brave and wise. He said just one word: "MAN!"

All the birds and animals followed him back into the woods. Bambi was at his side. They heard frightening roaring noises behind them as they ran.

Later, when Bambi and his mother were safely back in their
thicket, his mother explained.

"That was Man in the meadow, Bambi. He brings danger
and death to the forest with his long stick that roars and
spurts flames. Someday you will understand."

The months passed, and the days grew cool. Winter was coming.

One morning when Bambi woke up everything was covered with white. "It's snow," his mother said. "Go ahead and walk on it." Bambi stepped out and saw Thumper sliding on the frozen pond. "Come on," Thumper called. "The water's *stiff!*"

Bambi trotted onto the ice. His front legs shot forward, his rear legs slipped back, and down he crashed!

"That's okay," said Thumper, laughing. "We can play something else. Winter's fun!"

But winter was also a hard time for the forest animals. Food was scarce. Sometimes Bambi and his mother had nothing to eat but the bark on the trees.

One day, when it seemed there was no food left anywhere, Bambi's mother found a few pale blades of grass growing under the snow.

They were nibbling the grass when they suddenly smelled
Man. As they lifted their heads, they heard a deafening roar.
"Quick," said Bambi's mother, "run for the thicket."
Bambi darted away. He heard his mother's hoofbeats
behind him, then another roar from Man's guns. Terrified, he
ran faster.

When Bambi reached the thicket, his mother was nowhere in sight. He sniffed for her scent. There was nothing.

"Mother!" he called, racing wildly out into the forest. "Mother, where are you?"

The great Prince of the Forest appeared beside him.

"Your mother can't be with you any more," the Prince said. "You must learn to walk alone."

Bambi did not understand, but he knew he must listen to the great Prince. In silence he followed the old stag through the snowy forest.

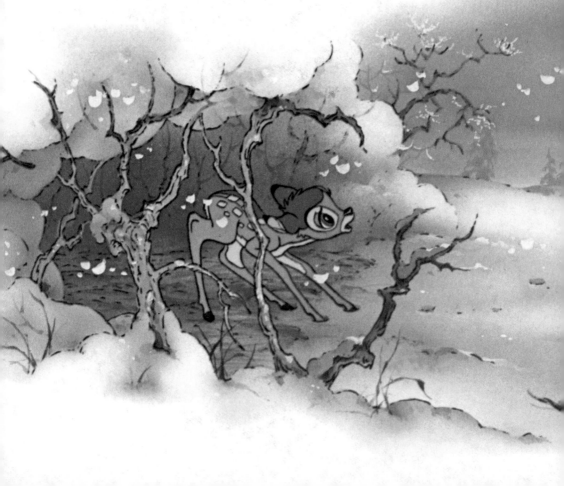

At last spring arrived. The forest was turning green and leafy. And Bambi was growing into a handsome buck.

One day Bambi met a beautiful, graceful doe in the woods. "Hello," he said. "Who are you?"

"Don't you remember me?" the doe asked. "I'm Faline." Gently, she licked Bambi's face.

Suddenly Ronno, a buck with big antlers, pushed his way
between them. He began to nudge Faline down the path.

"Faline is coming with me," he said.

Bambi charged forward and butted Ronno with all his
might. Again and again he and Ronno crashed into one
another, forehead to forehead.

A prong broke from one of Ronno's antlers, and he lost his balance. He fell to the ground, hurting his shoulder.

Ronno limped off by himself, and Bambi and Faline walked down the path together.

That night Bambi and Faline went out to the meadow and stood in the moonlight, listening to the east wind and the west wind calling to each other.

One morning in autumn Bambi sniffed the scent of Man
again. As he ran to warn Faline, he smelled something else,
too—smoke.

The old Prince came and said, "The forest has caught fire
from the flames of Man's campfires. We must go to the river."

Bambi turned to Faline. "Run!" he said. "Run to the river."
Faline raced off as Bambi and the Prince ran to warn the other
animals.

At last Bambi and the Prince struggled across the rushing river. When they were safely on the other side Faline came running to Bambi. They stood with the other animals on the bank and watched the flames destroy their forest home.

"When the forest is green again, I will be very old," said the Prince. "Bambi, you must take my place then."

Bambi bowed his head.

When spring came, green leaves and grass and flowers covered the scars left by the fire.

At the thicket, the squirrels and rabbits and birds were peering through the undergrowth at Faline and two spotted fawns.

And not far away was Bambi, the proud father and the new great Prince of the Forest.